MARUSHKA
AND THE MONTH BROTHERS

A Folktale Retold by
Anna Vojtech & Philemon Sturges

Illustrated by Anna Vojtech

NORTH-SOUTH BOOKS · NEW YORK · LONDON

Text copyright © 1996 by Anna Vojtech and Philemon Sturges
Illustrations copyright © 1996 by Anna Vojtech

Published in the United States by North-South Books Inc., New York.
Published simultaneously in Great Britain, Canada, Australia, and
New Zealand in 1996 by North-South Books, an imprint of
Nord-Süd Verlag AG, Gossau Zürich, Switzerland.

Library of Congress Cataloging-in-Publication Data
Vojtech, Anna.
Marushka and the Month Brothers : a folktale / retold by Anna Vojtech
& Philemon Sturges ; illustrated by Anna Vojtech.
Summary: A retelling of the Slavic folktale in which the Month Brothers'
magic helps Marushka fulfill seemingly impossible tasks which prove
the undoing of her greedy stepmother and stepsister.
[1. Folklore—Slavic countries.] I. Sturges, Philemon. II. Title
PZ8.1.V57Marj 1996
398.2'0947'01—dc20
[E] 96-21741

A CIP catalogue record for this book is available
from The British Library.
Typography by Marc Cheshire

ISBN 1-55858-628-8 (trade binding)
1 3 5 7 9 TB 10 8 6 4 2
ISBN 1-55858-629-6 (library binding)
1 3 5 7 9 LB 10 8 6 4 2
Printed in Belgium

For more information about our books, and the authors and artists
who create them, visit our web site: http://www.northsouth.com

ARTIST'S NOTE

In Czechoslovakia, where I grew up, people loved to listen to and tell stories. It was one of my family's favorite pastimes. I can still hear my mother's voice. . . .

"Marushka and the Month Brothers" was always my favorite. It's a very old folktale that has been told in Czech and Slovak villages for countless generations.

Years ago I hiked through the powerful and mysterious Tatra Mountains of Slovakia. There people still lived in beautiful log houses and dressed the traditional way. Friendly and proud, they were part of that rugged landscape. I felt that Marushka and the Month Brothers must be nearby. I knew then that someday I would retell and illustrate this story.

I would like to say a special thank-you to Philemon Sturges. It was a joy to work with him and to tell him about the customs of my country. He is not only a sensitive writer, but also an attentive listener. Now he knows that fragrant violets do blossom in Slovakia in March.

I'd also like to thank my husband, Roland Baumgaertel, as well as Phil Bailey, Susan Sherman, and others at Studio Goodwin Sturges for their encouragement and assistance. As soon as I can find the right kind of noodles and sheep cheese, I'll cook them a pot of halushky covered with bacon and melted bryndza.

ONCE UPON A TIME there was a girl named Marushka. She lived in a cottage near a village at the foot of the Tatra Mountains with her stepmother and her stepsister, Holena.

People in the village say that Marushka's warm smile could thaw a January day.

But it could not thaw Holena and her mother. They were jealous.

Her stepmother made Marushka work hard. She hoped hard work would make Marushka gnarled and wrinkled and take away her smile. She longed to be rid of her in spite of all that she did for them. But the harder Marushka worked, the more beautiful she became. Holena and her mother's envy grew, and gnawed away at their hearts.

One freezing winter day the snow drifted up against the door. Nonetheless, Marushka milked the cow, fed the pig and chickens, cut the wood, lit the stove, and cooked a hot pot of porridge.

Holena crawled out of her warm bed. "What a dreary day," she said. "Wouldn't it be nice to have violets to smell?"

"But it's winter. There are no violets," said Marushka.

"Find some," said Holena's mother as she pushed Marushka out the door. "And don't come back without them!"

Then Holena and her mother sat down by the stove and ate all the hot porridge.

Marushka stood in the icy wind. Then she struggled up the mountain through the blinding snow.

Far ahead she saw a light.

She headed for it.

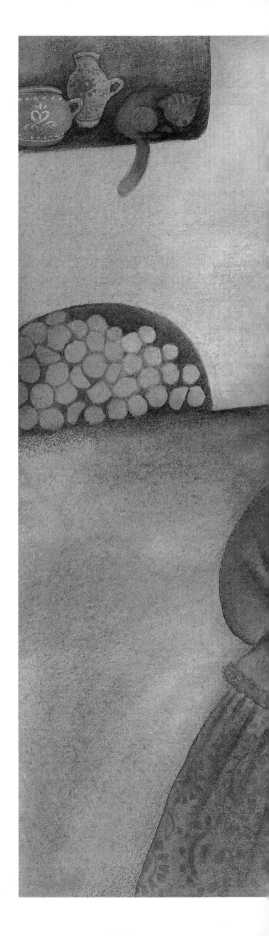

She came to a hollow. In the middle of the hollow was a ring of twelve rocks. On each rock sat a man. One rock was taller than the others. It was the throne. A small fire burned before it.

Marushka was numb. She stared at the fire.

"May I?" she asked the old man sitting on the throne as she held her frozen hands over the fire.

"Yes, my child," he said. "Do you know who we are?"

"I think you must be the twelve Month Brothers. I am Marushka."

"And I am Brother January. What brings you here?"

"My sister wants violets," replied Marushka.

"It's winter. There are no violets," he said.

"But please, may I stay by the fire till my hands are warm? I can't go home without violets."

Brother January stood up and handed the staff to his youngest brother, Brother March.

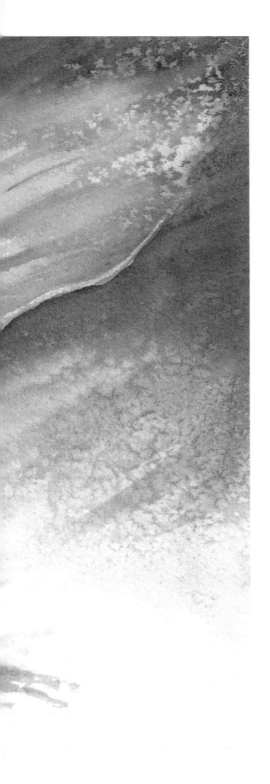

Brother March sat upon the throne. He waved the staff above the fire. The flames flared. The snow melted, the hollow became green, and violets blossomed in the grass.

"Be quick, Marushka," said Brother March. "I cannot let spring leave the hollow."

Marushka picked violets as fast as she could. Then she said thank you with a smile as warm as her heart and left.

"Why are you back?" Holena's mother demanded as Marushka opened the door.

"I have violets," she said.

The house was filled with the smell of springtime.

The stepmother stared at Marushka, and Holena grabbed the violets.

The next day was bitter cold. Wind-blown snow covered the windowpanes. Nonetheless, Marushka cleaned the kitchen, made the beds, and swept the cottage floor. Then she made a steaming pot of halushky.

Holena crawled off her cushion by the stove. "What a dreary day," she said. "Wouldn't it be nice to have strawberries?"

"Your sister wants strawberries! Get some for her," Holena's mother said as she shoved Marushka out the door. "And don't come back without them!"

Holena and her mother sat down by the stove, covered the halushky with bacon and cheese, and ate it all up.

Once again Marushka stumbled upward through the deep snow. When she came to the ring of rocks and the fire, her toes were frozen.

"May I!" she asked.

"Yes, my child," said Brother January. "But why are you back?"

"My sister wants strawberries," she said.

"But it's winter. There are no strawberries!"

"I know," she said. "But please let me stay a while. I can't go home without strawberries."

Brother January stepped down and handed his staff to Brother June. Brother June sat upon the throne and swung the staff above the fire. The fire flared high, and instantly the snow in the hollow melted. Blossoms bloomed, bees buzzed, the white flowers fell, and strawberries formed and grew red and sweet.

"Hurry!" said Brother June. "Summer must not escape from the hollow."

Marushka picked the strawberries. She said thank you with a smile as big as her heart and left.

"Why are you back?" Holena's mother demanded as Marushka opened the door.

"I have strawberries," said Marushka.

The house was filled with the smell of summer.

The stepmother stared at Marushka, and Holena grabbed the strawberries. Then she and her mother ate them all!

The next day the wind-whipped snow piled up to the eaves. Nonetheless, Marushka dug a path through the snow, fed the pig and chickens, cut firewood, stoked the stove, baked the bread, made a pot of cabbage soup, and started spinning.

Holena got up from her nap. "What a dreary day," she said. "Wouldn't it be nice to have juicy apples?"

"Your sister wants fresh apples! Get some for her," Holena's mother said as she threw Marushka out the door. "And don't come back without them!"

Holena and her mother sat down by the stove and ate all the bread and soup.

Marushka struggled into the bitter wind, stumbling up and up and up. Once again she headed for the light and approached the fire.

"Marushka," said the old man. "I can help you only one more time. What do you need?"

"Holena wants apples," she stammered. There were tears in her eyes. "I can't go home without apples!"

With that Brother January stepped down and handed his staff to Brother September. Brother September sat on the throne and swung the staff above the fire. The flame flared red, the snow melted, leaves sprouted, blossoms turned into green apples; then the leaves turned yellow and began to fall. The apples became large and red and juicy.

"Shake the tree," said Brother September.

Marushka shook it. An apple fell.

"Quickly, shake it again before autumn escapes the hollow!" he said.

She shook the tree again. Another apple fell. She picked up the apples and with a radiant smile said thank you to each of the Month Brothers as she left.

"Why are you back?" Holena's mother demanded as Marushka opened the door. "Don't tell me you have apples!"

"I have apples," she said.

The house was filled with the scent of autumn.

Holena and her mother stared at Marushka.

"Why didn't you bring us more?" Holena demanded. "Did you eat them all?"

"No, no," replied Marushka. "These are all I could get."

"Liar!" said Holena as she snatched the apples.

She bit into one. So did her mother. They had never tasted anything so sweet. They gobbled them down. They wanted more.

Holena put on her sheepskin coat.

"I'll get them myself," she said. "Then Marushka can't eat them." She grabbed a sack and went out.

"Holenka, my baby," her mother cried after her. "You can't go alone into the cold mountains. The snow is deep. There are wolves and bears. There might be a storm!"

But Holena paid her no heed.

The mountain was steep, the snow was deep, and Holena was cold. But she thought about those juicy apples and how happy she'd be when she had them all for herself.

Then she saw a light.

She found the hollow, the circle of stones, the fire, and the twelve Month Brothers.

She went right to the fire and stretched out her hands.

"Who are you?" asked Brother January.

"Never mind who I am, old man. Just get some wood and make this fire bigger!"

Enraged, Brother January stood atop the throne and waved his staff in an angry circle over the fire. There was a blast of cold air. The fire flickered. A terrible blizzard blew over Holena like a herd of wild white horses. She stumbled away.

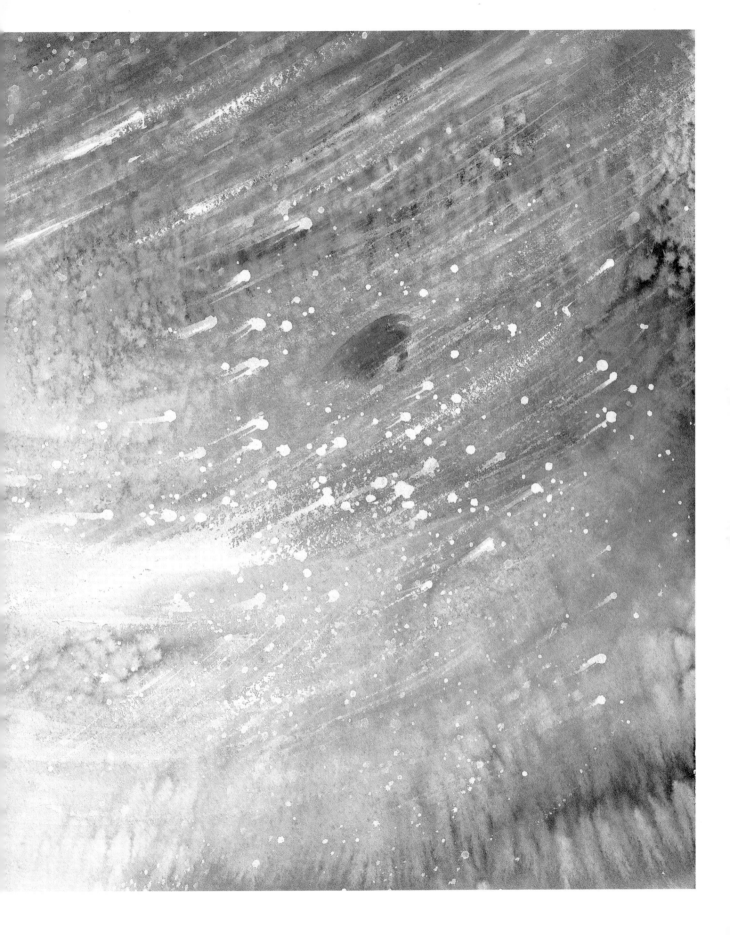

Holena's mother saw the sky turn black. She grabbed her sheepskin coat and fleece boots and ran out to find her daughter.

The storm was so bad that the people in the village said that devils were having a wedding feast. They locked their shutters and lit their prayer candles. They hid. The storm raged for days.

Marushka kept the animals fed, the stove lit, the food warm, and the house clean. She waited for Holena and her mother to return. But she waited in vain. They never came back.

On the first warm day of spring, Brother March scattered sweet-smelling violets in the grass beneath Marushka's window. On the first day that the summer sun shimmered high in the sky, Brother June covered Marushka's meadow with ripe red strawberries. On the first crisp autumn day, Brother September loaded Marushka's tree with so many juicy apples that the branches bent low. And the Month Brothers have done so ever since.